The LAST BLACK KING of the KENTUCKY DERBY

THE STORY OF JIMMY WINKFIELD

by Crystal Hubbard
illustrated by Robert McGuire

Lee & Low Books Inc. · New York

To Boogie. No one could ask for a better editor, muse,
confidante, and accomplice—C.H.

For Mom and Dad—R.M.

ACKNOWLEDGMENTS

I send my deepest thanks and gratitude to Liliane Winkfield Casey, Churchill Downs director
of publicity Tony Terry, author Ed Hotaling, Joe Drake, the Kentucky Derby Museum, Ed Gray,
Judy and Annette, the staff at the Lucius Beebe Memorial library, and my two-legged racing
encyclopedias Johnny and Jen Safrey.—C.H.

AUTHOR'S SOURCES

Casey, Liliane Winkfield. Personal interview by author. January 25, 2006.
Chew, Peter. *The Kentucky Derby: The First 100 Years.* Boston: Houghton Mifflin, 1974.
Clippinger, Don. "Black Jockeys, Derby Glories." *Thoroughbred Record*, May 1990.
Hotaling, Edward. "Black Jockeys Rode Into History." *Baltimore Sun*, February 6, 2000.
———. *The Great Black Jockeys: The Lives and Times of the Men Who Dominated America's First National Sport.*
     Rocklin, California: Prima Publishing, 1999.
———. "When Racing Colors Included Black." *New York Times*, June 2, 1996.
———. *Wink: The Incredible Journey of Jimmy Winkfield.* New York: McGraw-Hill, 2005.
Saunders, James Robert, and Monica Renae Saunders. *Black Winning Jockeys in the Kentucky Derby.*
     Jefferson, North Carolina: McFarland & Company, Inc., 2002.
Schmidt, Neil. "Black Jockey's Journey Spanned Different Worlds." *Cincinnati Enquirer*, April 29, 2002.
     http://www.enquirer.com/editions/2002/04/29/spt_black_jockeys.html.
Terrell, Roy. "Around the World in 80 Years." *Sports Illustrated*, May 8, 1961.

Text copyright © 2008 by Crystal Hubbard
Illustrations copyright © 2008 by Robert McGuire

LEE & LOW BOOKS Inc.
95 Madison Avenue, New York, NY 10016
leeandlow.com

Manufactured in China

Book design by Tania Garcia
Book production by The Kids at Our House

The text is set in Baskerville
The illustrations are rendered in oil

10 9 8 7 6 5 4 3 2 1
First Edition

Library of Congress Cataloging-in-Publication Data
Hubbard, Crystal.
   The last Black king of the Kentucky Derby : the story of
Jimmy Winkfield / by Crystal Hubbard ; illustrated by
Robert McGuire. — 1st ed.
      p. cm.
   Summary: "A biography of Jimmy Winkfield, who
battled racism and other obstacles on the road to becoming
one of horseracing's best jockeys and, in 1902, the last
African American to win the Kentucky Derby"—Provided
by publisher.
   ISBN 978-1-58430-274-2
   1. Winkfield, Jimmy, 1882-1974—Juvenile literature.
2. African American jockeys—Biography—Juvenile
literature. 3. Jockeys—United States—Biography—Juvenile
literature. 4. Horse racing—United States—History—
Juvenile literature. 5. Horse racing—Europe—History—
Juvenile literature. 6. Kentucky Derby—History—Juvenile
literature. I. McGuire, Robert. II. Title.
SF336.W475H83 2008
798.40092—dc22
[B]   2006039015

FOREWORD

Horse racing, "the sport of kings," enjoyed in Europe by royalty and the aristocracy, came to the shores of the United States with the earliest settlers. Races were recorded as early as 1665. At the time most horses of well-off landowners were cared for by slaves, so the slaves were usually assigned to be jockeys. Through horse racing these jockeys gained fame and in some cases freedom. One such man, Austin Curtis, began racing as a teenager in the 1700s and became so well-known that he was considered America's first professional athlete.

Horse racing's popularity and prestige continued to grow with the nation. On May 17, 1875, the Kentucky Derby—one of America's oldest premier races— made its debut. Of the fifteen jockeys who raced that day, fourteen were black, including the winner, Oliver Lewis. Between 1875 and 1902 black jockeys won fifteen of twenty-eight Derbys, and African American Isaac Murphy became the first jockey ever to win back-to-back Derbys, in 1890 and 1891.

It was during this reign of African American racing legends that a true king of the sport took center stage. Some knew him as Jimmy Winkfield. To others he was simply Wink.

Jimmy Winkfield in jockey silks

Jimmy Winkfield was a small boy with big dreams. Born in 1882 in Chilesburg, Kentucky, he was the youngest of seventeen children. His parents, poor sharecroppers, farmed a parcel of land owned by someone else. On the farm, all the children had to work hard. Although Jimmy was the smallest, he never let his size stop him from doing anything he set his heart to. He would carry the heaviest bucket, climb the tallest tree, chase the fastest chicken. Whether at work or play, Jimmy always gave his all.

What Jimmy loved best was riding horses. He was captivated by the big, powerful animals. After rushing through his chores, Jimmy would sit for hours watching the thoroughbreds parade between local horse farms and the racetrack in nearby Lexington. Sometimes he would hop on one of the workhorses, riding it bareback, pretending to be a jockey. Atop a horse, Jimmy felt big and powerful too.

Horses seemed to love Jimmy right back. When he
talked to them and gently stroked their muzzles, the
horses bowed their heads as if they were listening.
When Jimmy rode, he didn't need to speak at all.
The click of his tongue, a twitch of his hands,
or pressure from his knees was all it took for the
horse to understand what he wanted it to do.
Jimmy dreamed of riding horses for the
rest of his life and becoming a great jockey,
like Isaac Murphy. Ike Murphy was the
best of the best. His picture and news
of his races were always in the papers.
Ike Murphy gave Jimmy hope that
his own dream was possible.

As a teenager, Jimmy began spending time at the racetrack
on weekends. He became so well-known by the stable hands that
they gave him the nickname Wink. Eventually Wink was offered a
job as an exercise rider and stable hand at a racetrack in Latonia,
Kentucky. Part of his pay was room and board.

Living at the track, Wink learned even more about horses and
began studying the jockeys too. He watched how they handled
their horses, the way they talked to them, how they raced them.
When Wink saw the jockeys sitting proudly in the winner's circle
dressed in their fine colored silks, he knew he wanted to be there
one day himself.

In the spring of 1898, Bub May, a horse trainer and son of the mayor of Lexington, hired Wink as an exercise rider for his horses. A few months later, in August, Wink got his first chance to race. May, unable to afford an experienced jockey, asked Wink to ride his horse Jockey Joe at the Hawthorne Track outside Chicago. Wink was only sixteen years old. He had gone from exercise rider and stable hand to jockey in less than a year. This race could be his big break.

Wink grew nervous and excited as the day of the race approached. He had seen Jockey Joe blazing around the track during morning workouts, so he knew he had a good, fast horse. Now it was up to Wink to prove he was a skillful jockey.

When the barrier was sprung, Wink and Jockey Joe bolted. They fell to the back of the pack, but gradually Jockey Joe fought his way up. By the time they reached the far turn, there were only five horses in front of them. Wink pushed Jockey Joe hard, all the while searching, searching. Then he found what he was looking for—an opening to move Jockey Joe to the front of the pack.

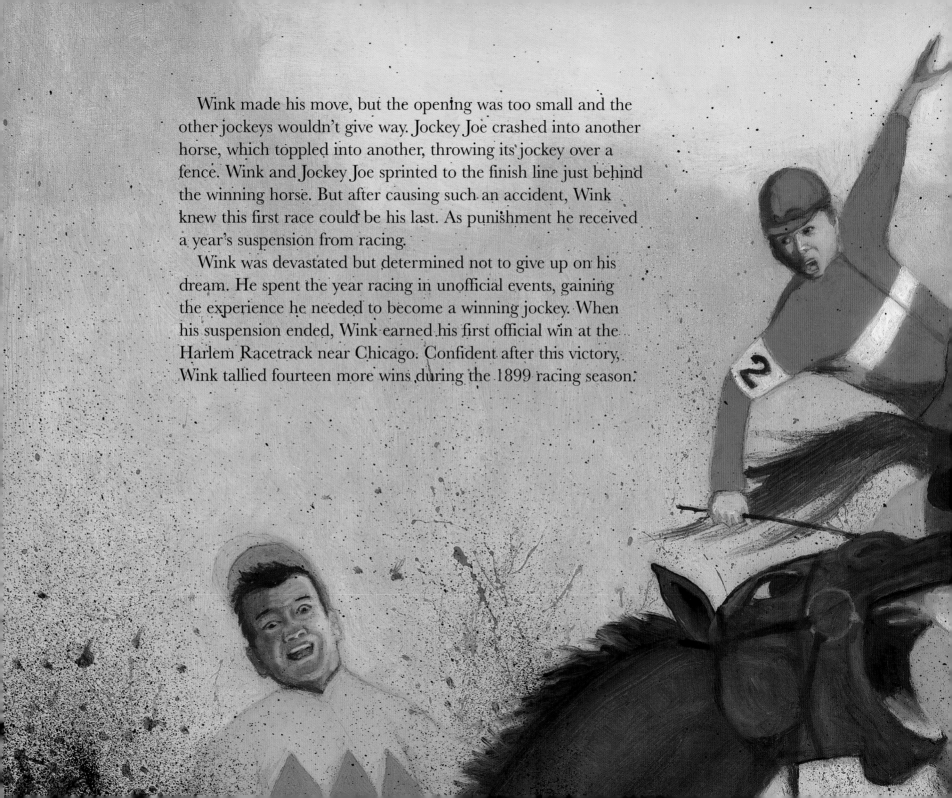

Wink made his move, but the opening was too small and the other jockeys wouldn't give way. Jockey Joe crashed into another horse, which toppled into another, throwing its jockey over a fence. Wink and Jockey Joe sprinted to the finish line just behind the winning horse. But after causing such an accident, Wink knew this first race could be his last. As punishment he received a year's suspension from racing.

Wink was devastated but determined not to give up on his dream. He spent the year racing in unofficial events, gaining the experience he needed to become a winning jockey. When his suspension ended, Wink earned his first official win at the Harlem Racetrack near Chicago. Confident after this victory, Wink tallied fourteen more wins during the 1899 racing season.

The next year Wink broke into horse racing's big leagues. He got his first chance to race in one of the country's most prestigious races, the Kentucky Derby. Wink wanted nothing more than to win the Derby. The race would be a chance for his brothers, sisters, and friends to see him ride in his home state. His parents had died years earlier, but Wink knew they would be watching over him, wishing him a win.

Saturday, May 3, 1900, was Derby Day in Louisville, Kentucky.
People walked from miles around to watch a race that would last
little more than two minutes. Ablaze in orange and blue silks, Wink
rode out onto the track atop his mount, Thrive. Wink had ridden
the horse a few times before the race, so he knew Thrive was a strong
animal with a cool head. Wink was sure he and Thrive could pull off
a victory.

Staring into the crowd of spectators, Wink had never felt so alive.
He eyed the track. Just one-and-a-quarter miles stood between him
and a Kentucky Derby win.

Time seemed to stand still as the horses were positioned at the starting line. Finally the signal rang out, and the horses were off. Wink acted fast, pulling Thrive in close to the rail, hoping to make the trip around the track as short as possible. Approaching the first turn, Thrive was fourth.

At the three-quarter mark Wink hunkered down, dug in his heels, and began his charge. Fans screamed wildly. Panting through clouds of dirt and the spray of horse sweat, Wink powered Thrive into third. Closing in on the finish line, they began to battle for second place. Neck and neck with the other horse, they crossed the line.

Wink and Thrive placed third. It wasn't the win Wink had hoped for, but he took comfort in knowing a third-place showing in the Derby put him on the way to becoming a great jockey.

Just as Wink's career was taking off, racial conflicts began to emerge in the horse-racing world. Black jockeys were offered many of the best mounts, and white jockeys were jealous. Wink became a victim of this jealousy three months after racing in his first Derby.

During a race at the Harlem Racetrack, a white jockey named J. O'Connor purposely crashed Wink and his horse into the rail. The horse ended up with two broken ribs, and Wink suffered serious leg injuries. He could have been killed.

It took months for Wink to recover, but by April 1901 he was
back in top riding form and on his way to his next Kentucky Derby.
This time Wink would ride His Eminence, one of the country's best
racehorses. Wink was nineteen years old and the only black jockey
in the race. This was his second chance at a Derby win, and he was
more determined than ever.

Confidence surged through Wink as he sat astride His Eminence
at the starting line.

When the signal sounded, Wink responded instantly. His Eminence
shot into the lead. Nothing could stop them. By the final turn, they
were ahead by three lengths. The snorts of His Eminence, the
wind whistling past Wink's ears, and the pounding of his own
heart drowned out the sounds of the other jockeys driving
their horses faster. Pressing on, Wink and His Eminence
sailed over the finish line.

Wink had won the Kentucky Derby!

Wink stood before the audience, proud to be the most recent in a long line of jockeys to have won the Derby. When the winner's garland of roses was placed on His Eminence, tears of happiness filled Wink's eyes.

After his Derby triumph, Wink continued to build his reputation as one of America's premier jockeys. He won races throughout Kentucky, Illinois, Tennessee, New York, Louisiana, and Ohio.

With one hundred sixty-one wins during the 1901 season, Wink felt more prepared than ever heading into his third Kentucky Derby, slated for May 3, 1902.

Major Thomas Clay McDowell had asked Wink to ride one of his two horses, either Alan-a-Dale or The Rival. Nash Turner, a white jockey, was also riding for McDowell and would get first pick of the two horses. Alan-a-Dale had weak legs and The Rival was in good shape, but Wink had exercised both horses and saw a special spark in Alan-a-Dale. Even with weak legs, the horse was a hard worker that wouldn't quit. Wink devised a plan to make sure Turner picked The Rival.

For a month before the Derby, Wink slowed Alan-a-Dale in his workouts. He never allowed the horse to run the mile and a quarter faster than The Rival. When Derby Day arrived, instead of taking each horse out for a ride himself, Turner chose to stand trackside and just watch the morning workouts. Again Wink slowed Alan-a-Dale's workout. The Rival appeared to be the faster horse, so Turner chose to ride him in the Derby.

When the race began, Wink and Alan-a-Dale shot from the starting line. The other jockeys were sure the weak-legged horse would tire after such a quick start. They were right. Approaching the backstretch, Wink felt Alan-a-Dale's knees wobble.

Wink clung desperately to the lead. His slight body tensed with the effort it took to keep fifteen hundred pounds of horse running at top speed. The Rival and the other horses were closing in. Reacting quickly, Wink steered Alan-a-Dale to the right, just enough to force the other horses into the deeper sand surrounding the race path. It didn't stop them, but it slowed them enough to keep Alan-a-Dale in the lead entering the homestretch.

Sweat stung Wink's eyes. He gritted his teeth and tuned out all the stomping and snorting around him. Leaning forward, he pushed Alan-a-Dale harder. The horse gave him everything it had. Wink and Alan-a-Dale crossed the finish line as the rest of the pack thundered past in a blur of browns, blacks, and rainbow-colored silks.

When the dust settled and the crowd quieted, Alan-a-Dale was declared the winner by a nose. Wink had won his second Kentucky Derby in a row, making him the only back-to-back Derby winner since Ike Murphy.

Wink was a genuine star by the 1903 racing season. With a streak of twenty-two victories earlier that year, he was feeling confident when he mounted a horse named Early in the Kentucky Derby on May 2. Early was the favorite, and with Wink on board a win seemed like a sure thing.

Wink wanted this victory more than any other. No one had ever taken three Derbies in a row—not even Ike Murphy. When the horses were lined up at the starting tape, Wink was so anxious that he caused a false start.

After a second lineup, the horses were off! Wink pushed Early hard, bolting past three other horses. Starting so quickly was risky, but it had worked for Wink in the past.

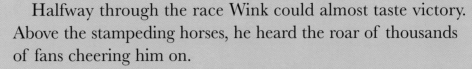

Halfway through the race Wink could almost taste victory. Above the stampeding horses, he heard the roar of thousands of fans cheering him on.

Wink urged Early to go faster, but Henry Booker aboard Judge Himes caught up in the homestretch. Eye to eye, stride for stride, muscle to muscle, Early and Judge Himes fought for the finish. Then, suddenly, Early's breathing grew harsh and his neck became damp with sweat. Wink's heart sank. He knew his horse had nothing left.

Judge Himes crossed the finish line first, less than a length ahead of Early. Instead of cheers, Henry Booker was met with the stunned silence of thousands of spectators who had expected to see Jimmy Winkfield win his third Derby in a row. No one was more disappointed than Wink. He realized that he had made his move too soon. He had thought too much about the victory and not enough about the race.

After 1903, economic problems drove many racetracks in the United States out of business. As opportunities began to dry up, jockeys became more competitive, vying for the few available mounts. Racial tensions between jockeys increased. Soon Wink and other black jockeys were forced out of racing by white jockeys who wanted their mounts and white horse owners who chose not to use black jockeys.

Despite hard times Wink eventually found work with Jack Keene, a Kentucky man who trained horses in Poland and Russia. Keene asked Wink to ride for Mikhail Lazareff, owner of one of Russia's largest racing stables. In Russia Wink won the Emperor's Purse, which led to races all over Europe, riding the horses of Russian czars, Polish princes, and German barons. While in Europe Wink married and had a family. He was happy and glad to be racing again, but part of him always missed the dirt of the tracks back home.

EUROPE

Wink made a few attempts to return to the United States, but times had changed too much. Black jockeys, once the kings of horse racing, were no longer welcome at American tracks. Wink's 1902 victory would be the last Derby win ever by an African American jockey.

In 1930 Wink retired from racing and settled his family on a twelve-acre horse farm in Maisons-Lafitte, France. He spent his later years on the farm doing what he loved best—working with horses. Whenever Wink thought back on his long journey from Chilesburg to Maisons-Lafitte, he didn't dwell on the bad times. Wink knew he had been blessed. The small boy from Kentucky had lived a big life.